NATURE'S PAINTBOX
A SEASONAL GALLERY OF ART AND VERSE

May you always find joy in the art around you!

Patricia Thomas

Patricia Thomas

illustrated by

Craig Orback

M Millbrook Press • Minneapolis

For Mother and Dad,
who taught me to see the art around me
—P.T.

For Jessica, a Connecticut girl,
who taught this California boy a few
things about the seasons
—C.S.O.

Nature sketches
WINTER,
I think,
in pen and ink . . .
black and white;
sharp and clear and fine;
no colors to blur the line . . .
or maybe,
just a bit at a time . . .

berries on a bush;
    cardinals on a branch;
a red mailbox flag
      winking a cheery hello,
    snuggled under
its caps of snow;
    a snowman's carrot nose,
      a holly wreath
with a red velvet bow;
a pink sunset,
    glowing behind hilltop trees—
      every lacy twig outlined.

Mostly though,
it's black and white,
so you can see all the patterns . . .
all the tiny, tiny, tiny

patterns . . .
boot prints;
weed shadows;
birds floating high in a winter sky;
snowflakes,
bright white—
no two ever quite alike—
or so they say.

(It is true, no two alike ever landed on a mitten.

Now, if you catch them on your tongue . . .

well, it's hard to tell. They melt away.)

White snowy day;
        black snowy night;
winter is done in
    pen and ink . . .
            black and white.

And then . . .
Nature draws
SPRING
in pastel chalk,
dotting crocuses along a walk;
forsythia against a wall . . .

drawing them all in
warm-as-sunshine colors;
gentle baby colors;
blurry, furry,
baby-chick, baby-duck colors . . .
fresh-green-fuzzy, baby-leaf,
baby-fern colors . . .
soft colors, showing slowly,
perhaps so the surprise
of color in a black-white world
won't hurt your eyes.
A tulip here, a hyacinth there.
Blue violets push the snow aside.
Time to wake up,
daffodils decide—
and in a dash of yellow,
off they dance, along a path . . .
beside a fence.

Suddenly,
before you can
blink...
there are blossoms
everywhere...
blossoms,
peach and white
and pink;
fluffy, puffy,
pillowy,
billowy,
spun-sugar,
cotton-candy
blossoms;
blossoms;
blossoms.

Sometimes
a day is clouded
pussy willow gray
and streaked with
blue-silver rains—
washing streets
and windowpanes
and rooftops . . .
watering crops
of umbrellas
that grow
on sidewalks below . . .
until by and by,
a rainbow
sends all the colors
arching across the sky.

I guess no one will mind
if a few puddles—
fine for splashing—
are left behind . . .
along with drops that drip on your nose
when you close your umbrella . . .
plip . . .
plunk . . .
plop.
Spring is done in pastel chalk.

And then . . .
Nature paints
SUMMER
in watercolors—
reds, greens, yellows, purples, blues . . .
pure, clear,

nearly see-through-them hues…
as hot as hot dogs
or as cool as diving
in a swimming pool…
as wet as ocean spray,
flashing, splashing in;
bright as a buttercup,
glowing butter-yellow
under your chin.

Summer colors sparkle…

shine…sizzle…dazzle…
there's no time for
subtle shadings…
gentle…slow.
Summer colors have places to go…
baseball and picnics in the park…
parades and fireworks when it's dark.

Summer's blue is
bluest sky...
or blue, blue morning glories
that try to tumble
from their window box
and catch the purple hollyhocks.

Summer's green is
greenest trees,
waving deep green
shadows in the breeze...
or a green frog
that winks a yellow eye,
snapping at a
shiny green
dragonfly.

Summer's red is
red geraniums in red pots;
and red strawberries—
lots and lots.
In splashes,
dashes, spots and dots;
in rings; on wings
and things that sing—
summer colors, one by one,
are clearly busy having fun!
In watercolor is
how summer's done.

And then . . .
Nature works
AUTUMN in oils . . .
coils of color,
brilliant, twining, vining, seen as
redorangepurplebronze
indigogoldgreen . . .
chasing round and round . . .
in a game of tag with
crimsonrustyellowtancranberrybrown.

Fire colors…that sparkle…
crackle…
blaze…
dance with sky colors—
bluegray smoke; bluepurple haze—
and earth colors,
warm, dark, mellow…
curled, whirled,
brushed in a rush of
scarletorangebluegray
purplebrowntanyellow…
sandtan cornstalks, row on row…
a goldorange jack-o'-lantern's glow.
unending blendings…
shade on shade,
tone on tone.
Autumn colors
are never known to play alone.

Heaped and stacked
and draped in boxes,
baskets, crates...
yellowrosegold
purpleblueblackgreenred...
apples, pears,
plums, grapes
are spread
in all sorts of sizes...
textures...
shapes.

Leaves blow...
go tumbling,
twirling
swirling,
falling...
pile them high...
run...
spin...
jump in...
let them fly!
Autumn is
done in oil...
rich, bold
redrustbronzescarlet
cranberryorangetanbrown
yellowgreengold!

And then
Nature somehow seems to find a camera—
the old-fashioned kind—
and, with a laugh, snaps a photograph…
not black and white…
nor color, quite…
but one with a sort of mellowy,
birch-leaf yellowy, oak-leaf brown,
meadow-grass tan, warm, sepia glow—
like pictures taken long ago.
You have to look quickly, though.
A click…
a quick gust of wind…
in a wink it's hard to tell
what the photograph had been…
and then…
Nature draws
WINTER
in pen and ink…

Craig Orback worked in four different media to render this book. Winter was done with Micron ink pens on bristol board. Color was added using the computer program Adobe Photoshop. Spring was rendered with pastels on watercolor board that was toned with a wash of watercolor. Pastel pencils were used for detail. Summer was painted using tubes of watercolor on cold press paper. And for fall, the artist used oil paint on watercolor board that had been gessoed and toned using acrylic paint. The transition spreads joining two different media were done in Photoshop.

The artist wishes to thank Olivia and Samantha Pess for doing such a great job of modeling for the illustrations.

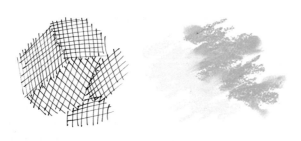

Text copyright © 2007 by Patricia Thomas
Illustrations copyright © 2007 by Craig Orback

Millbrook Press, Inc.
A division of Lerner Publishing Group, Inc.
241 First Avenue North
Minneapolis, MN 55401 U.S.A.

Website address: www.lernerbooks.com

Library of Congress Cataloging-in-Publication Data

Thomas, Patricia, 1934–
    Nature's paintbox : a seasonal gallery of art and verse / by Patricia Thomas ; illustrated by Craig Orback.
        p.   cm.
    ISBN: 978–0–8225–6807–0 (lib. bdg. : alk. paper)
    1. Seasons—Juvenile poetry. 2. Children's poetry, American.
I. Orback, Craig, ill. II. Title.
PS3570.H5755N38 2007
811'.54—dc22   2006035079

Manufactured in the United States of America
1 2 3 4 5 6 – JR – 12 11 10 09 08 07